Baby bear goes to the Farm

Lorette Broekstra

BRIMAX

For Glenn, Wendy,
Timothy and Nicholas

First published in Great Britain in 2002 by Brimax
An imprint of Octopus Publishing Group Ltd
2-4 Heron Quays, London E14 4JP

Originally published in Australia in 2002 by Thomas C. Lothian Pty Ltd

ISBN 1 85854 488 2

Printed in Spain

One day a letter arrived for Baby Bear. It was from Farmer Bear. His dog Rosie was missing and he needed help on the farm.

“Please, may I go?” asked Baby Bear.
“Of course,” said Papa Bear. “I’ll take you there.”

Papa Bear drove Baby Bear to the farm.
"I'll pick you up at the end of the day," said Papa Bear.

Baby Bear found Farmer Bear near the haystack.
"I'm glad you could come," said Farmer Bear.

“What would you like me to do?” asked Baby Bear.
Farmer Bear gave Baby Bear a list.

“**1**. Milk the cow,” read Baby Bear.
He milked the cow and filled **one** bucket

with creamy white milk.

“**2**. Brush the donkeys,” read Baby Bear.
He brushed the **two** donkeys.

“Heehaw,” they said, “that felt good.”

"**3**. Feed the geese," read Baby Bear.
He fed the **three** geese.

“Honk! Honk! Thank you,” they said.

"**4**. Bring the horses to the field," read Baby Bear.
He let the **four** horses out of the stable

and brought them to the field.

"**5**. Round up the sheep," read Baby Bear.
He rounded up the **five** sheep

and put them in their pen.

"**6**. Collect the eggs," read Baby Bear.
He collected **six** eggs.

“Cluck. Cluck. Hello, Baby Bear,” said the chickens.

"**7**. Gather the corn," read Baby Bear.
He picked **seven** ears of corn.

They looked delicious.

"**8**. Check the piglets," read Baby Bear.
He counted — one, two, three, four, five, six,
seven, **eight** piglets.

They all seemed fine.

“**9**. Pick some apples,” read Baby Bear.
He picked **nine** ripe, red apples.

Baby Bear had finished all the jobs on his list.
He went to tell Farmer Bear.

But on the way, he heard a yapping sound.

It was coming from behind the haystack.
Rosie! He'd found Rosie.

He'd found Rosie and **ten** baby puppies!